DATE DUE

1-30-11			

Demco

scrut
poems by george roberts

scrut

poems by george roberts

Holy Cow! Press • MINNEAPOLIS • 1983

An earlier version of "scrut dreams how to do it" appeared in *A Coloring Book of Poetry for Adults* (vol. 2) published by Vanilla Press. Permission to reprint is gratefully acknowledged.

Copyright © 1983 by George Roberts

ISBN 0-930100-10-7

Library of Congress Number: 82-081349

Cover photographs and photo of author by Vicky Deger

First Printing

All rights reserved. No part of this book may be reproduced without permission from the publisher.

Typesetting by Annie Graham & Co., Iowa City, Iowa

Printed in the United States of America

Publisher's Address:

Holy Cow! Press
Post Office Box 618
Minneapolis, Minnesota 55440

Principal Distributor:

Bookslinger
330 East 9th Street
Saint Paul, Minnesota 55101

This project was made possible in part by a grant provided by the Minnesota State Arts Board from funds appropriated by the Minnesota State Legislature and from the National Endowment for the Arts. Publication is made possible by a grant from the National Endowment for the Arts, a Federal agency.

table of contents

- 11 his name
- 12 scrut
- 13 scrut's genesis
- 14 highschool
- 15 scrut reacts
- 16 lament
- 17 scrut thinking about his friends
- 18 scrut dreams how to do it
- 19 scrut at the tower
- 20 gym class   scrut tries the rope climb
- 21 as news of the party spreads
- 22 halloween   the hydrant dare
- 25 scrut   daring himself to be worthy
- 27 scrut has two mothers
- 28 scrut's own voice comes toward him
- 32 scrut discovers science fiction
- 33 scrut denies the woman in himself
- 34 scrut gets marty crowe for social studies
- 36 when no one is home
- 38 scrut finds a spot on the sidewalk
- 39 walking home from school
- 41 as stage manager for the school musical
- 42 after scrut completes his biology homework
- 43 looking out his window
- 44 after careful consideration
- 45 what scrut knows and does not know
- 46 when school is out scrut plays
- 47 a short walk to the rootbeer stand
- 49 he begins to know what he lacks
- 50 scrut walks in the woods
- 51 county fair
- 53 scrut dreams himself into a hole
- 55 scrut goes out for track
- 57 while dissecting frogs in biology
- 58 poetry
- 59 scrut delivers his valedictory
- 60 all he did

*for Art Froehle
always there
to read the poems*

his name

one part thumbnail
gouging a blackboard

one part tire   hubbed
in mud   spinning

the unspeakable question
of mirrors
two parts

one part boxcars
wrenching the night
in the eastside yards

the chugging engine of desire
three parts

three parts stumbling
stumbling

one part blood
in its noisy tunnel

one part scribbling
on an old lunchbag

scrut

spends his days in his mind
the dark place under his old baseball hat

cameras whirling day and night

until guilt cancels the bright stamp
of his movie set life

and leaves him hushed
like the gaudy travel stickers
on an unclaimed suitcase
at the greyhound depot

scrut's genesis

first   the child's dream
           plunging into dawn

           a rock dropped into a still pond

           eyes refusing the dazzling thump of light
           banging off bruised water

next   the reproach of toys

           dust glowing on the jar of marbles
           his prized baseball cards   fading
           in the ruined cigar box

then   the safe skin of his room burns
           like the flame of a small incision
           on each eyelid

           he welcomes the darkness
           under his bed

finally   far off   an engine whines
           the night smells like a candle
           gone out

on a cracked bench
at the busstop near school
a child sits   alone

i am the child
i am scrut

staring into the growing night
knowing i will take the bus
knowing it will take me
into my nightmare

highschool

while the school's star athletes
snap down beer on country roads
and later stumble into basement parties
(where once   to prove a boast
donna mccarthy   for the briefest of moments
removed her blouse)

scrut does his homework
thinks about the justice of letter jackets
and pronounces another final judgment
on his friends

all the while wishing
he shared their easy way
with books and rules
with colt 45 malt liquor
and with the electric skin
of donna mccarthy

scrut reacts

---

when scrut woke
he laughed

on the floor   his history
books   his latin translations
teased a windy flutter
from his throat

                        and the laugh turned
                        to pain

on the wall
his crazy crayon sun
grew childish in his eyes

                        and the pain went deep
                        into his confused voice

his carking smile
scraped its knuckles
on the raw edge
of his guilt

                        the voice balked
                        at its own name

the sky (squeezed
through the narrow window
of his laughter)
       turned blue
        turned black

so scrut lay back
like a twisted sheet

and wondered

lament

my old red schwinn had a carrier over the back fender
on your first day   gail   i would ride you to school
you would hold my side with one hand and balance
our lunch sacks in the other   your legs dangling
outside the flashing spokes   we would talk and laugh
if it should suddenly rain   i would give you my jacket

but by three years old your heart had grown too large
for your body   i never rode you on my bike   i
never took you to school   i am afraid to go there
myself now   and my heart is the reverse of yours
sister   it is growing smaller

scrut   thinking about his friends   turns to stone

while mike seery stretched for higher and higher grace
on the trampoline in the gym
while heimermann replaced the headgasket in his '38 chevy
scrut watched

while cheerleaders practiced in the hall after class
while couples strolled out of movies holding hands
while mike ahern sold pokerchips in his basement
       during school
scrut watched

while donna stood by her locker and combed her hair
scrut watched

when everyone was gone
and there was nothing to watch
scrut went down to city hall
to look at that fusty statue
on the lawn

the one whose name
no one could remember

scrut dreams how to do it

by staying awake all night

by leaving his jacket unzipped in winter

by spying the brief whisk of thigh
as girls step onto the bus

by holding the breath and tensing the muscles

by carrying a clean comb and thumbing its music

by risking a stroll past houses of girls
he might meet in the dim light of the tower

by admitting his shoes want to run away

by staring at his bewildering self
in the mirror

by refusing to park with carol edwards

by accepting the tangled parachute   of his secret
parts   fusing him to the tumbling night

scrut at the tower

> teenagers now have a place
> to be themselves: the tower
> —*daily herald*

he chooses indian posture
in the corner booth   and plays chess
while everyone around him dances

over the chesspieces he watches
lissome sheri heil   her body sliding
like silk inside her clothes

his stomach knots at her grace
and he smothers this anger as scorn
for the shrill music blaring at him
like the plant whistle in the morning

still   he wonders what would please her
argues himself out of asking her to dance
pleading his awkward   feet his thick
tongue

instead he sits   legs going numb
absently offering a king's gambit
his mind more with sheri's dancing
than his feet will ever be

waiting for something inside her
to   something at least to turn her eyes
toward him

hoping   hoping somehow she will see
beyond the ragged metaphor of dance

and   oh   how brilliant
to know how to play chess

**gym class
scrut tries the rope climb**

near the top
nearer

now   and nearer

now   legs kicking

*son of a bitch
it must be now*

the rope leaps
like fire
past his burning
breath

      the dim halls
      between classes
      the dark halls
      the night

days later
sparks of hemp
still stab the soft pads
of his upturned hands

throbbing almost
almost

as news of the party spreads
scrut attempts several letters to donna

i think i know why you did it
not for any dirty reason either
i am the oldest in my family
and i change a lot of diapers
i wish i had been there
i would have understood

      i have never spoken to you
      but in the fine light of certain stars
      the words wait

      how shall i begin?

was it quiet?
i know some of those creeps

i hope they didn't laugh

      your hooves have stamped outside my window
      i have seen you there the last three nights

      the dark hair of your mane
      the soft hair of your neck
      shimmers each hour
      within my clothes

you are courageous
honest about your body
i mean it

if you unbuttoned your blouse
for me
no one would know

**halloween
the hydrant dare**

---

1. no eggs put behind the garage to rot
   no shaving cream   no soap

   something holds them back
   says no   to getting things ready

   and now   as a ghost of winter
   invades their breath   and little folk
   scurry through the falling dark
   scrut and heimer and heimermann walk out
   into the gaudy geometry of this night

   wheels turn inside their bellies
   they are loose   open

   ready

2. they amble under a frosted moon
   caught in low branches   until
   the dull gleam of a pipe wrench
   forgotten on a neighbor's step
   gives them direction

   the hydrants

3. winded   laughing
   they sit in the tower grill
   stomachs aching with the joy of it

   imaginations racing
   with the trail of streaming hydrants
   they left behind

    they do not speak
    but gloat   and gulp air

4 devonna and michelle know something is up
    and slide   like cats   into the booth

    heimer and heimermann know they will walk these girls home
    and fall all over eachother to spin the tale

> *first*
> *we stood/still as/statues*
> *taking it all/in*
>
> *later/we ran*
> *from the foaming/water*
> *lifting/into the/street*

    the lights and sounds in scrut's head
    go dead as a tilted pinball machine at the arcade

    his ears burn
    like candles in a pumpkin

5 moons leap in the girls' eyes
    and the five go out
    to find the wrench

6 but this time there is no magic
    no spark leaping the dark space
      between them
    and the shadow of a car   waiting
    freezes them in its spotlight

        the running/the hedge leaping/the darkness
        brings back/for a moment/the quick breath
        of surviving

but when they meet in sumner park
there are only four

devonna squirming in the squad car
gives all the names   almost before
she catches her breath

7 in school the story grows
   but scrut knows   as heimer and mann know
   the glory is flat

   the captain's words
        one more time   boys
        and your asses will be racked up
        on meat hooks over at the plant
   still ringing in their ears

   but ringing louder   their own
        yes sir
   cancelling what was left of the private
        joy of those first dozen hits

   and now   sitting in the back of algebra class
   their separate thoughts of how it could have been
   drain away like the last drops of water
   as the hydrants were closed

**scrut   daring himself to be worthy of donna
poses a test   and learns another lesson instead**

---

your dark eyes would glow
if you knew   if you knew

and the gloating voices of friends
would be still   if they heard

      with eyes clamped shut
      i wait in weeds beside the road
      where 218 curves twice
      near the lumberyard
            once is enough   once is enough
            more than once is crazy

      choking down bile for courage
      until the sound of tires fades

            once is enough   once is enough
            more than once is worthless

      then
      breath like burning hay
      eyeballs full of steam
      i cross that highway
      on my knees

      and tumble   singing   into the ditch
      as earthquake eyes fall open
      on the other side

            once is enough   once is enough
            more than once   impossible

your trembling face would glow
and their voices would grow quiet

but the words of this song are mine
like the photographs i found   in the attic
that lift me out of my life

lift me   out of my life

scrut has two mothers

and like a telegram in the night
the hand of this second woman reaches out
to claim the child she left   for adoption
fifteen years earlier

her name is guilt
she finds him in wold's drugstore
flushed with first discoveries
of the magazine rack

> the torn blouse in *captive woman*
> the hero's rescue in *real man*
> each page of *saga* not enough
> wanting more more more more
> until the verdict of flesh rings
> in his ears

mother guilt   in a simple print dress
peers in at him from outside the display window
she is everyone in town

scrut learns a new word   her name
her bouquet of gestures turns to fists
balled tight as closed eyes

he knows she follows him   shadows him
as he rides his bike home
in the gauzy yellow afternoon sun
trying to think about baseball

**scrut's own voice comes toward him
disguised as someone he cannot name**

---

slouched in the plaid chair by his window
a snarled parachute of the day's defeats
drops round him

each class each word spoken each thought
another penny on his bitter tongue

he holds his breath
until he tastes the dark honey of exhaustion
until each cell flares up   a point of light
in his darkness

he holds his breath
until the words   like fists
disperse the agony of vision
into stars

> *do you want the shadows of trees*
> *falling across city streets*
> *to hide your immeasurable guilt?*

> > *they will   they will*
> > *ask them*

> *do you want the moon*
> *rubbing its wings*
> *on the edge of this dark*
> *to help you grow taller?*

> > *it will*
> > *reach toward it*

scrut sits up
his bones end over end
like streams in spring

do you hope the sliding rectangles of light
offered by passing cars to the blank mirror
of your window
will teach you to be correctly dressed
in the piercing eyes of your friends?

    they will
    watch them

do you want your winter skin
calling from the splintered leap
of telephone poles
to silence your father's voice?

    it will it will
    direct it

he goes on listening
the fingers that are his fist
closing on air
closing on dark air

    do you see your own confused gestures
    revealing the face of one
    who will love you?

    they can   they will
    make them

    do you wait for the first wind   announcing
    a coming storm to bring you   her name?

    it will come
    listen

> *and are you anxious to scatter moons*
> *inside the yielding frame*
> *of her night?*

> *do it*

scrut twists in his chair
each hour of the night shrinking
like a noose

> *do you think mike ahern's famous*
> *pornographic playing cards will give you*
> *the secret knowledge*

> *they will*

> *take them*
> *look*

the voice is the hum of bees
in the hot sun of his head

> *do you want the morning light*
> *the orange bones of the sun*
> *to catch fire   to fall*
> *on your teachers' eyes*
> *lighting your face*
> *in their favor?*

> *it will*
> *ask*

even when the voice falls still
scrut   unable to move
listens

and in the aching bend of morning
as he wakes   he remembers
this voice   a glimmer

but the flame in him stops
against his tongue
and there is nothing more

scrut discovers science fiction

somewhere nearby the sand dreams of lapsing
atom by atom   into glass
something comes out of this book
and carries me off

i am left swimming for days
in cloistered waters

when i come ashore   i carry a small dial
and the beach has turned into windows
memory lights up a stretch of road
i turn the arrow to 'past'
and follow

      i untake all my algebra tests
      and unlearn not knowing how to dance

      i undo all the excuses i have wound myself into
      and unlearn how to walk

      unlearn how to crawl

      unlearn how to cry

scrut denies the woman in himself

she is soft
without guise

and he closes this door
a thousand times a day

scrut gets marty crowe for social studies

and while his gray voice drones on from the front desk
a slate sky mumps across october windows

the afternoon becomes a cloudy river
begging its way past bending trees

scrut fingers the ragged skin around his knuckles
his eyes catch on a single twisting leaf
tied   by last memory of summer
to its branch outside the classroom

> *practice today should be hard as rocks*
> *the cold makes even good hits sting*
> *and crowe   that bastard   keeps us*
> *out there twice as long*
> *the day before a game*
>
> *fisting up his face*
> *snapping his cap to the ground*
> *and cracking the raw blue air*
> *with his cursing and roaring*
> *til these eyes water*
> *and these ears ring*

near his window a silent bird
leaps into the bruised air
an empty branch quivers

> *the real thing quiets him*
> *because we usually win*
>
> *so friday nights he broods*
> *and paces the sidelines*
> *red face and bullwhip voice hidden*
> *from those in the stands who retell*
> *tales from the practice field and think*
> *they own not only us   but him*

the window tilts a quarter inch
and scrut   jarred loose from his daydream
lands back inside the classroom

marty crowe is reciting poetry
just as ted heimer said he would

> *the way crowe's voice turns   like a leaf in the sun*
> *the way his eyes glaze   into a damp middle distance*
> *and float up   toward the ceiling*
>
> *like a man happy to be drowning*

scrut surrenders his breath
to the current of words

the spine of an oak leaf snags on a fallen tree
at a bend in the red cedar river

his football jitters fade   then rush out
like a dream on waking   and scrut feels
something inside himself   break loose

because here is a teacher   a teacher
who needs a way out as much as scrut does

and knows it

**when no one is home
scrut takes a self portrait
with a polaroid**

the empty house magnifies his sounds
his ears strain   for the doorslam
the footfall   downstairs

half remembered nursery rhymes slide
out   and in   on his breath

outside his window   the sky
clouds over

       in this moment rinsed with silence
       he puts on the loops of his mother's earrings

       his father's sportcoat   old matchbooks in the pocket
       hangs like an aging shadow   from his shoulders

first drops of rain tick   against the window

       scrut leans toward the lens
       pouting his lips into confessions
       of his longing to be beautiful

the earth gives up its heat
the thunder   just then   drums
sending him the hundred miles
between himself and the film

       he drops all his costumes
           all his disguises

       the camera trembles to accept his light

scrut stares at the ghost of his double life
flapping the ragged sheet of its nakedness
in the storm's glare

with a cockeyed smile
he folds the photo
into his wallet

unsure about keeping it
unwilling to throw it away

**scrut finds a spot in the sidewalk
where money regularly appears**

do not let it matter
if crazy elmer is laying out quarters again
or if a child lost her lunch money

do not question the burning coins
that appear like mushrooms after warm rain

do not search for answers in the dark corners
   of the garage
or snap a look at the window across the street
   for a face disappearing behind the curtain

say nothing
simply bend to the coins
slip them into your pocket
and head up to the drive-in
near maloney's station

where elaine fink is the car hop
and the whole football team hangs out
after practice

**walking home from school scrut imagines his secret
initiation into the knights of the laughing dog club**

---

there
piece of red twine
knotted round the broken elm

pretend not to notice
(cameras hidden everywhere)
the slightest nod will do

keep walking

      password: this is the morning of windled snow
 counterphrase: a white map folds along the horizon

         route: bob past the plant like a beer can in the river
                  zigzag through the dark along the curve in 14th street
                  pause where the iron fence corners the cemetery
                  hug yourself like the thief his loot

         place: under the slide in todd park
     & time: when the moon slips behind a cloud
                  at midnight

        orders: no matter the torture
                  reveal nothing

          plan: hunker down in the shadow of the slide
                  scrape the wormy archives of soil
                  near the ladder

                  read the words
                  then forget them

keep walking   keep walking

    the message: when the dew glistens
                        and smells like winter
                        the clock will strike thirteen

    the answer: the darkness is only that
                        the day   its other name

keep walking

    the action: wait for the plant whistle at dawn
                        count the streetlights flickering out
                        go home and sleep

keep walking   keep   walking

**as stage manager for the school musical
scrut takes on the job of keeping everybody happy
and so begins telling jokes**

---

the first   at the readthrough   so bad
the cast's groans jolt him
toward an unexpected pleasure

(did you hear the one about the farmer with two horses?)

the stage is set
and scrut assumes it   briefly   each day
savoring the moans and jeers and sighs
like the juice of a winesap apple
dribbling down his chin

(what's the difference between a swan and a necklace?)

the play jumps and spartles toward readiness
scrut busies himself backstage   and smiles

(there was this blind racecar driver who)

in the gut tight flurry of opening night
the queen hovers near paralysis behind the curtain
the cast ready to take its cue from her

(how did the chicken get its mail?)

and when the play is over
when the audience is pleased and gone home
when the cast party is going strong at betty's

then scrut   listening to his heels click
on the empty stage   strolls to the dressing room
and in his best john wayne voice   says to the mirror

        sometimes its easier   sonny   to play the fool
        than to work so hard at dodging the bullet

after scrut completes his biology homework
he leans into the exit door of the public library
and drifts into the early night   murmuring
something like a prayer

---

let me please walk home without meeting anyone who knows me

let me stroll white marble stairs   polished by my passing
and never come to a door

let me be invisible

let me please be the floating island
in the wide part of the river near the plant
and let ducks climb up from the water to sleep
on me when they are tired of children and children's bread

let me have as many eyes as the sea scallop in my science book
and let me please   just once   close those eyes without fear
everything will be the same when i open them

let me learn to watch the curve ball
all the way to the sweet part of my bat

let me please encounter the dream of pleasure
i know nothing about

let the gypsy perfume of lilacs soaking this night
like the darkness around a streetlamp
soften the cuticle of regret
i carry with me

let my path glimmer   briefly   behind me
like the snail's single road

let me be morning grass   and draw the ringing breath of sunlight
down into the soft earth   where dark and not dark invent
their startled balance   around my roots

**looking out his window on sunday morning
scrut considers the question of grace**

there are things in this world worth going down on my knees for
   a handful of mushrooms glistening in the early sun
   donna's smile across the classroom
   a perfect squeeze play in the bottom of the ninth

there are things in this life that ought to be called holy
   but i would rather find them in a line of poetry i can't forget
   than in the papery words of a sunday sermon

is it the vision of donna's skin
the pearl light of her breasts
the hard rock of lust i keep tripping over?
or the way wind comes before a storm   turning
   leaves over   showing their silvery undersides?

the well chosen word on the page
is the first brick in a private cathedral

but   god   i am not ready
for any of this

**after careful consideration
scrut attends the boy scouts' masquerade
as a beatnik poet**

and they will think
oh   this one just stepped out
of a greenwich village basement

you can tell by the mirrored
sunglasses worn in the dark
and the sportcoat over blue jeans

they will lean a bit toward me
especially the girls   but some guys too
when i sit on the floor near my candle
and read from this book of 17th century poetry

the cowboys and arabs   the football hero
and the tiger   will bunch together
at the far end of the room and whisper

and i will go home electric
because i dressed up
into something like a dream
of my real self
and tried it on
and liked it

what scrut knows   and does not know
about elmer the moon man

---

that he can   while doing those slurping noises
with his mouth   make a polarizing lens
from the cellophane of a cigarette pack

that he believes   and will stop anyone on the street
to stammer that the slightest unexpected turn of the head
will send us flying off into deepest space

that for a quarter   he will show you   the moon
through his prized and battered telescope
the loose and jumping fish that are his hands
trying to point   trying to point

that though scrut's friends shout *moon face*
and *piss head* from across the street
elmer will go on examining the extra hole in his belt
the one he put there with a nail so he could cinch it
tight enough

but why elmer's stumbling voice
held back by an unwilling tongue
    ya got any any any cigar any cigar boxes?
silences scrut's own greeting

or why that right hand quivers and curls
back toward its own wrist

or what thing elmer carries in that ragged gunny sack
as he lumbers heavy footed up main street
looking for something that is never there

are questions scrut does not want to answer

when school is out scrut plays summer ball

he rides his bike   each day alone   to the field
no matter
he stands away from the others   toeing the dirt
   knowing his name will be last called
no matter   it's all right
he's having trouble hitting the curve ball
   for distance
the mask and chest protector hang   like halloween

but none of these things matters any longer
because today ike joel pitched a no-hitter
and scrut's hand still stings from catching
the game

>   *that baseball hanging   one minute   big as a pie*
>   *out there near ike's face*
>   *and the next   blazing   smack   into my mitt*
>
>   *batter after batter*
>   *inning after inning*
>   *i crouched behind home plate and watched*
>   *something near perfect as i can imagine come*
>   *toward me   and not veer away*

now scrut sits on his front steps in early evening
rubbing oil into the deep mouth of his glove
hardly noticing friends who drive by
hardly thinking about donna

he can't stop stretching his swollen fingers
or peering   amazed   at the lines in his red hand
any more than he can stop the glowing throb
or the night falling round him like watered silk

can't stop any of this
and does not want to

not ever

a short walk to the rootbeer stand

two coins in my pocket
slap against my thigh

a quarter for the you know what
a dime to phone the news

> *(would you care to attend*
> *the homecoming dance with me?)*

old man winslow in t-shirt and slippers
sits on the boarding house porch   like a judge
drilling me with his watery eyes

> *(you're going to the dance*
> *with me   aren't you?)*

what kind of dress will she wear?
and where will we go after?
the oak leaf?   the riveria?
east side lake?

> *(i hope no one else has asked you   baby*
> *because you'll have to disappoint them)*

slowly   walk slowly to the counter
order and take a stool
wait for her to finish a couple
   more orders

> *(when you have a minute   elaine*
> *i'd like to ask you something)*

pretend there are not so many cars
parked under the glaring lights
concentrate on the sugary foam
spilling over cold mugs

> *(will you please go to the ah*
> *homecoming dance with me?)*

deftly take a napkin and blot the spilled rootbeer
off your shirt before she notices
ignore the leering faces behind windshields

> *(who are you going to the dance with?)*

focus   grab your breath
watch her butt move
as she carries out
another tray

> *(i'd really like to take you*
> *to the homecoming dance)*

why won't the wind leave my hair alone?
why did i wear this light green shirt?
the stains show up like spotlights

> *(i don't suppose   you'd consider*
> *going to the dance   with me)*

walk away before she says hello
try try try to seem as calm
as when you came

flip the dime
into winslow's yard

he begins to know what he lacks

if only i could
   curl my hands into fists
   after the city championship game
   and bloody these knuckles
   on some eastsider's cheek or jaw
   without worrying about my own face

if only i could
   take the 218 curve at ninety
   without breathing hard
   or carry the ultimate switchblade
   bulging in my pocket
   without expecting the sirens
   the handcuffs

if only i could begin
   to down the can of malt liquor
   without thinking of hangovers
   or palm the ace
   the trump and the deuce
   of ahern's deck

if only i could begin correctly
   be first ice edging around a rock
   in the river near the ballpark

     or slide   unnoticed
     into her darkened room
     a fiend
     with crystals in his eyes

scrut walks in the woods at the edge of town

the dayblind mole slants his tunnel
   toward the surface
without sound   the owl leaves his branch
scrut touches himself there   and there

dusk circles the small clearing
the mole   savoring his final inch of dirt
   breaks through   to open air
the owl drops   through layers of fading light

scrut still as gray rock
lungs shrunk to fishribs
lodged in his chest
breath short/and helpless
in his mouth

> *donna donna donna*
> *eyes sparking the early night*
> *why was i not at that party*
> *to claim you?*

his fist goes limp
the mole's pink snout   and the owl's blood-
red talons   melt
into the ruby clouds of evening

county fair

1   august
    first week in august
    green and yellow august
    when death hides itself inside the trees

    scrut grows restless at the changing
    the distance shrinks between his house
    and the fairgrounds

2   *looky looky here*

    his eyes blaze red and gold
    circus neon squeezed down to the size
    of the sparkling stone in salome's navel

              it's all on the inside
              every bit of it

    mother guilt steps near him
    twisting his stomach like a wet towel

              hoochie-koochie girls
              step right up

    he holds back in the crowd
    calliope music whirling through both
    of his lives

              last chance tonight
              just a dollar
              gets you more than a peep

3   scrut stands alone in the midway
    his forehead a wrinkled newspaper
    night breezes rippling the coloring book poster
    of the incredible woman-man
    who comes each august into his life

    and when she walks out of the tent
    wearing blue jeans and a satin cowboy shirt
    scrut can only stare

        hi honey
        you like the show?
        was i good   hum?

    scrut's tongue knots worse than elmer's ever did

        you're her him ah
        i didn't recognize you with your ah
        without your ah ah

    the smile dissarms him completely

        i didn't see your show
        you were great
        i'm sure you

    and she is gone
    into the slow dancing light
    of the merry-go-round's exit sign glow

    then scrut wanders home
    believing they could be friends
    that he   she   is the nicest person
    you'd ever want to meet
    just with both of 'em
    down there

scrut dreams himself into a hole

i could be the one
who sinks the ball from midcourt
in the last second of the game
and who speaks   crowd screaming
of a team victory

i could be the one
who sees what is not there
who describes the mechanics
of the cloud chamber
in physics class

i could be the one
who assumes the stage at assembly
who speaks generously
until everyone believes
he is free of doubt

i could be the first in our school
to break the ten second hundred

i could be the one
for whom the band stops playing *paper moon*
as i sweep into the school dance
wearing a dinner jacket with velvet lapels
donna   demure and elegant   holding my arm
   with both hands

i could be the one
remembered after graduation
by freshmen who imitate my walk
or carry their hands like mine or wonder
how scrut would have said this or that

i could be the one
who survives a jungle plane crash
returning years later   honored graduate
for the children to admire the scars

scrut goes out for track

1 *the tape breaks*
curls away from breath
bursting   like gold   from his lungs

                        scrut pushes himself
                        into his baggy sweatsuit

there is a trophy in school
with his name on it

                        he walks to the practice field
                        carrying the red spiked shoes

the tape breaks
across his chest

                        his lungs burn
                        as the second lap begins

from the stands
donna's arms lift
in the light

                        the season of loneliness
                        of training   begins

his hands come up
above his head

the tape snaps

2 all winter
   scrut has dreamed
   in slow motion

spent his days listening
to cheering crowds

now he is alone
as each of his friends is alone
in the cool sun of false spring

mouthing the coach's words in his mind
in time to his feet crunching the track

> *how much pain*
> *are you willing*
> *to take*
> *for the glory*
> *of our old school?*

3 seery and brown and wedding are runners
they hold the secret of floating on air
dooley lofts the shot forty feet
his set face allows nothing less
hackenmiller jumps like a deer

scrut knows his place is not here
but in his winter dream
where he need only endure the crowd
pressing round him at the finish line

still   he counterfeits the motions of training
until a stabbing under his ribs   melts
the bright snow of his other life

and leaves him jogging   for no reason
around an empty cinder track

while dissecting frogs
in biology class
scrut discovers the intricacies
of the scooped neckline
in his lab partner's dress
───────────────────────────

oh madame curie
oh louis pasteur

oh ponce de leon
and christopher columbus

you have nothing on me today

poetry

when there is moon
clear sky of stars
and new snow covers the ground
i get into the old green chevy
and drive out into the country
to be lost

i close one eye
to gauge the moon's pitch
turn off the lights
and swell with the landscape
leaping round me

i drive into the snowy woods
of my imagination
wearing the cold like a new skin

the memory of maps disappears
and i sense the perfection
of the hunted animal

every silence in the world
settles onto my tongue

scrut delivers his valedictory
to the locker room mirror

i succeeded in school
because it was the only place left

i looked for approval from adults who did not know me
because i saw the candles flickering
   in my parents' eyes

i never asked the question of names on the phone booth wall

i never finished the equation
if a step on the stair is a fist in the heart

these memories my heart has failed to hold in
make their way back under my skin
ache through my body

       these hills exist   far as i can see
       i stand for years   rooted to their slopes
       giving them names i recognize as seasons
       each time i close   my eyes

all he did

in the way the flame of a match
settles after its first sulphur flare
the walls become remote

his hands remember
gripping the burning rope

                                        all scrut did   is look

there is no wall switch
for the light that washes him

the mist on the glass
while he watches
beads into cool rivers
in the lines of his face

                                        all scrut did   is look
                                        in the mirror

the rivers of his face bear him
down   into his childhood dream
where he holds his breath
and looks up into the sun's refracted light

until he learns to breathe underwater
until he enjoys privileged entrance
into a private place

and long after the dream fades
long after the match burns out
scrut floats   weightless
in this space

                                        all scrut did   is look
                                        in the mirror   and see

                                        himself

George Roberts was born in Chicago in 1943 and grew up surrounded by the Illinois woods west of that city. He spent his adolescence in a small town in southern Minnesota and now shares a house and a life with his wife and two children. He generally divides his time between writing and teaching. His two books include *the blessing of winter rain* (1976) and *night visits to a wolf's bowl* (1979).

NORMANDALE COMMUNITY COLLEGE
LIBRARY
9700 FRANCE AVENUE SOUTH
BLOOMINGTON, MN 55431-4399